Dear Parents and Educators,

Welcome to Penguin Young Readers! As parents and educators, you know that each child develops at his or her own pace—in terms of speech, critical thinking, and, of course, reading. Penguin Young Readers recognizes this fact. As a result, each Penguin Young Readers book is assigned a traditional easy-to-read level (1–4) as well as a Guided Reading Level (A–P). Both of these systems will help you choose the right book for your child. Please refer to the back of each book for specific leveling information. Penguin Young Readers features esteemed authors and illustrators, stories about favorite characters, fascinating nonfiction, and more!

L. Frank Baum's
The Wonderful Wizard of Oz

LEVEL **4**

GUIDED READING LEVEL **N**

This book is perfect for a **Fluent Reader** who:
- can read the text quickly with minimal effort;
- has good comprehension skills;
- can self-correct (can recognize when something doesn't sound right); and
- can read aloud smoothly and with expression.

Here are some **activities** you can do during and after reading this book:
- Creative Writing: Imagine you are a journalist covering the story of Dorothy's adventure in Oz. Don't forget to ask who, what, when, where, and why questions. For example, "Who did you meet on your trip?" and "Why was the Wicked Witch after you?"
- Descriptive Words: A descriptive word is one that points out a specific characteristic of someone or something. The author of this book uses a lot of descriptive words to show us the world of Oz and the characters Dorothy meets. For example, the Tin Man is "rusty," the Lion's teeth are "sharp," the forest is filled with "horrible" beasts, and the ditch they cross is "deep and dangerous." Reread the story, pointing to any descriptive words you see.

Remember, sharing the love of reading with a child is the best gift you can give!

—Bonnie Bader, EdM
   Penguin Young Readers program

*Penguin Young Readers are leveled by independent reviewers applying the standards developed by Irene Fountas and Gay Su Pinnell in *Matching Books to Readers: Using Leveled Books in Guided Reading*, Heinemann, 1999.

To my father, Walter Hautzig,
the wizard of music—DH

For Mom and Dad,
who first took me to Oz—RR

Penguin Young Readers
Published by the Penguin Group
Penguin Group (USA) Inc., 375 Hudson Street, New York, New York 10014, USA
Penguin Group (Canada), 90 Eglinton Avenue East, Suite 700, Toronto, Ontario M4P 2Y3, Canada
(a division of Pearson Penguin Canada Inc.)
Penguin Books Ltd, 80 Strand, London WC2R 0RL, England
Penguin Ireland, 25 St Stephen's Green, Dublin 2, Ireland (a division of Penguin Books Ltd)
Penguin Group (Australia), 707 Collins Street, Melbourne, Victoria 3008, Australia
(a division of Pearson Australia Group Pty Ltd)
Penguin Books India Pvt Ltd, 11 Community Centre, Panchsheel Park, New Delhi—110 017, India
Penguin Group (NZ), 67 Apollo Drive, Rosedale, Auckland 0632, New Zealand
(a division of Pearson New Zealand Ltd)
Penguin Books, Rosebank Office Park, 181 Jan Smuts Avenue, Parktown North 2193, South Africa
Penguin China, B7 Jaiming Center, 27 East Third Ring Road North,
Chaoyang District, Beijing 100020, China

Penguin Books Ltd, Registered Offices: 80 Strand, London WC2R 0RL, England

Text copyright © 2013 by Deborah Hautzig. Illustrations copyright © 2013 by Penguin Group (USA) Inc. All rights reserved. Published by Penguin Young Readers, an imprint of Penguin Group (USA) Inc., 345 Hudson Street, New York, New York 10014. Manufactured in China.

Library of Congress Cataloging-in-Publication Data is available.

ISBN 978-0-448-45588-4 (pbk)   10 9 8 7 6 5 4 3 2 1
ISBN 978-0-448-46508-1 (hc)   10 9 8 7 6 5 4 3 2 1

PENGUIN YOUNG READERS

LEVEL
FLUENT
READER
4

L. Frank Baum's The Wonderful
Wizard of Oz

adapted by Deborah Hautzig
illustrated by Robin Robinson

Penguin Young Readers
An Imprint of Penguin Group (USA) Inc.

Dorothy lived in a farmhouse on the Kansas prairie with Uncle Henry, Aunt Em, and her dog, Toto. The prairie was dusty, gray, and flat. One day was the same as the next. Dorothy dreamed of going someplace where the colors were bright and surprising things happened.

One afternoon, the sky became very dark. There was a sharp whistling in the air.

"It's a cyclone!" cried Uncle Henry.

"Hurry, Dorothy!" shouted Aunt Em. "Run down to the cellar!"

But Dorothy didn't get there in time, and a strange thing happened. The house spun around three times . . . and rose into the air with Dorothy and Toto inside.

"Toto, we are in the middle of the cyclone! Oh dear. What will happen when the house falls? We'll be dashed to bits!"

But nothing bad happened. The house kept flying, and soon Dorothy fell fast asleep.

Dorothy woke to a great bump. The house was not moving, and it wasn't dark anymore. She ran to the door and opened it. Dorothy cried out in amazement at what she saw.

There were huge flowers and fruit trees. Rainbow-colored birds sang and fluttered.

Dorothy saw a woman dressed in a sparkling gown. She wore a hat with bells around the brim, which tinkled as she moved.

"Welcome to the land of Munchkins!" said the woman.

"What are Munchkins?" asked Dorothy.

"The little people who live in this land. And I am the Good Witch of the North."

"But I thought witches were mean and ugly," said Dorothy.

"Only the bad ones. Thank you for killing the Wicked Witch of the East!"

"I did not kill anyone!" cried Dorothy.

"Your house fell on her," said the woman. "That is the same thing. See? There are her feet sticking out!"

Dorothy looked. Indeed, sticking out from under the house were two feet in silver slippers.

"Once there were four witches in Oz, two good and two bad. Now there is only one bad one left: the Wicked Witch of the West."

Suddenly the Munchkins shouted and pointed. The dead witch's feet were gone. Nothing was left but the silver slippers. The Good Witch gave them to Dorothy.

"Wear them," she said. "They have a magical charm."

The shoes fit Dorothy perfectly.

"Thank you," said Dorothy. "You are all so kind. But how do I get back to Kansas?"

"What is Kansas?" asked the Good Witch.

"It's where I live. It's very beautiful here, but I want to go home."

"Go to the Emerald City to see the Wizard of Oz. Maybe he can help!"

"How do I get there?" asked Dorothy.

"You must walk. Just follow the Yellow Brick Road," said the Good Witch.

Then she twirled three times and was gone! Dorothy said good-bye to the Munchkins and started down the road with Toto at her side.

Soon she came to a cornfield. There sat a scarecrow high up on a pole.

"How do you do?" said Dorothy.

"Not well at all," said the Scarecrow sadly. "I am stuck on this pole. Can you help me?"

Dorothy lifted him off the pole easily.

"Thank you!" said the Scarecrow. "If I had a brain, I would have been able to think of how to get down myself."

"You haven't got a brain?" asked Dorothy.

"No, just straw. No brains at all."

Then Dorothy had an idea.

"Come with me to see the Wizard of Oz. Maybe he can give you some brains!" she said.

"Oh, I'd love to!" said the Scarecrow. They set off together.

Soon they came to a forest. There stood a woodman, all made of tin. He tried to speak, but his jaws were too rusty.

"You poor thing!" cried Dorothy. She found an oilcan and oiled his mouth.

"Oh, I'm so lucky you came," said the Tin Man. "I haven't moved in more than a year! Can you oil my arms and legs, too?"

So Dorothy did.

"Where are you going?" asked the Tin Man.

"To the Emerald City to ask the Wizard of Oz to send me home," said Dorothy.

"And to give me some brains," added the Scarecrow.

"Do you think the Wizard could give me a heart?" asked the Tin Man.

"You have no heart?" exclaimed Dorothy.

"No. I can't be happy without one!"

"Come with us," said Dorothy. "I'm sure the Wizard can help you!"

"Oh, thank you!" said the Tin Man, and they all skipped down the Yellow Brick Road with Toto at their side.

Soon they entered a deep forest.
They heard a loud roar! A lion leaped
onto the road. He knocked down the
Scarecrow and hit the Tin Man. Then
he went after Toto and showed his
sharp teeth.

"Don't you dare bite Toto!" cried Dorothy, and she slapped the Lion on the nose. The Lion burst into tears!

"I didn't bite him!" said the Lion.

"No, but you tried to!" said Dorothy

angrily. She was surprised to see that the Lion kept weeping.

"Why, you are nothing but a big coward!" she said.

"I know," said the Lion sadly. "A lion is king of the forest, so all the animals think I am brave. But I know I am really a coward. I will never be happy if I don't find some courage."

Dorothy and her friends whispered to one another. They felt very sorry for the Lion.

"Come with us to see the Wizard," said Dorothy. "Maybe he can give you some courage!"

"And, please, stop crying," said the Tin Man. "If you cry, I'll cry, too. Then I'll rust again!"

So Dorothy, the Scarecrow, the Tin Man, and the Cowardly Lion went down the Yellow Brick Road together with Toto at their side.

Dorothy and her friends did not have an easy journey. They were chased through the forest by horrible beasts with bodies like bears and heads like tigers.

They had to ride on the Lion's back to cross a deep and dangerous ditch.

And they barely escaped from a field of deadly poppies that could have made them sleep forever!

At last everyone noticed a green glow in the sky. It was the Emerald City! They were so happy, they ran the rest of the way.

The Yellow Brick Road ended at a huge, gleaming gate studded with emeralds. Dorothy rang the bell, and a little man appeared.

"I am the Guardian of the Gates. Why have you come here?" he asked.

"We are here to see Oz," said Dorothy.

The man was shocked. "But no one has ever seen the great Oz!" he said.

"We've come *such* a long way," pleaded Dorothy. "The Good Witch of the North sent us. She even gave me these silver slippers!"

When the man saw the slippers, he
said, "Very well. I will take you. But first,
put these glasses on. The Emerald City
is so bright, it will blind you."

He was right. The green streets
and houses sparkled. Men sold

green popcorn and green lemonade.

Finally Dorothy and her friends came
to the palace and entered the throne
room. In the center was a strange sight:
a huge head with no body, no arms, and
no legs. Its voice was like thunder.

"I am Oz, the great and terrible! Who are you, and why have you come?"

"I am Dorothy, the small and meek, and this is Toto. We want to go home."

"I am a scarecrow, stuffed with straw. I have come for some brains."

"I am a cowardly lion, afraid of everything! Please give me some courage."

"I am a woodman made of tin. I was hoping you could give me a heart."

There was a long silence. Then Oz said, "I will grant your requests. But first you must earn them. Go and kill the Wicked Witch of the West."

"But how?" cried Dorothy.

"You must find out for yourself. Now go!"

Far away the Wicked Witch
of the West was looking out
her castle window. She had
only one eye, but could see
for miles around. When she
saw Dorothy and her friends,
she was so angry she tore out
her hair.

"I will destroy them!" she shrieked.
First she sent her servants, the Yellow
Winkies, to catch them. But the Winkies
were not brave. As soon as the Cowardly
Lion roared, they ran away!

Next the Wicked Witch sent her band
of winged monkeys. The monkeys grabbed
the Tin Man, then the Scarecrow, then the
Lion. Finally they got Dorothy and Toto.

When the Witch saw the silver slippers, she was furious. She knew they had magical powers and that Dorothy could not be harmed while she wore them. So she put Dorothy to work cleaning the castle and locked Dorothy's friends away.

"Curses! How can I get those shoes?" the Witch cried. "I have to find a way!"

Then the Wicked Witch thought of a trick. She used an invisible stick to make Dorothy trip and fall so that one of the silver slippers flew off.

"Hee hee!" cackled the Witch. "Some day I'll get the other one!"

"You wicked thing!" screamed Dorothy. She picked up a pail of soapy water and threw it at the Wicked Witch.

The Witch shrieked with fear, and

Dorothy watched her in amazement. She was melting!

"See what you have done?" wailed the Witch. She melted into a gray heap. Soon there was nothing left of her but a spot on the floor—and the silver slipper.

Dorothy was thrilled! She put the shoe back on and ran to free the Lion, the Scarecrow, and the Tin Man. Toto, too, of course!

Dorothy and her friends raced back to Oz to tell the Wizard what they had done.

"We've killed the Wicked Witch!" said Dorothy. "Now you can keep your promises."

"Let me think it over," said Oz in a trembling voice. "Come back tomorrow."

"But that's not fair!" cried Dorothy.

The Lion roared angrily, and Toto ran away. He tipped over a screen in the corner of the room. Behind it stood an old, bald man.

"Who are you?" cried the Tin Man. He held up his ax.

"I am Oz. Please don't hit me!"

"You are a very bad man," said Dorothy.

"No, my dear," said the man in a shaking voice. "I am just a bad wizard."

"What about the brains you promised me?" asked the Scarecrow.

"You don't need brains," said Oz. "You learn things every day!"

"That may be true . . . but I still want them."

So Oz took off Scarecrow's head and filled it with bran mixed with pins and needles.

"There. Now you have *bran*-new brains."

"What about Lion's courage?" asked
Scarecrow.

"You have lots of courage," Oz told
the Lion. "It's not cowardly to be afraid.
True courage is facing danger even when
you're scared!"

Oz gave him something green to drink.
"When it's inside you, it will be courage."

The Lion lapped it up.

"Now I feel full of courage!" he roared.

"What about my heart?" said the Tin Man. Oz smiled sadly and said, "Hearts can be broken, you know. That makes people very unhappy."

"But I still want one!" cried the Tin Man.

Oz knew that he had a heart already. But he cut a hole in Tin Man's chest and tucked in a soft, red silk heart.

"Is it a kind heart?" asked the Tin Man.

"Oh, very," said Oz.

Dorothy was so happy for her friends!
But then her eyes filled with tears.

"What about sending Dorothy home?"
asked the Scarecrow.

"I have a balloon. I will take her there
myself," said Oz. "Climb in, Dorothy!"

But Dorothy could not find Toto in time. The balloon took off, leaving her behind. Dorothy began to weep. Her friends tried to comfort her, but it was no use.

Suddenly the Good Witch of the North appeared. "Your silver shoes can take you home," she said. "If you had known their power, you could have gone home the day you arrived!"

"I'm glad I stayed to help my friends," said Dorothy. "But I am ready to go."

"Then click your heels three times."

First Dorothy kissed her friends good-bye. Then she held Toto in her arms, clicked her heels, and said, "Take me home."

WOOOSH! Dorothy sailed through the air and landed with a great bump. There were Aunt Em and Uncle Henry.

"Where have you been?" they cried.

"In the Land of Oz," said Dorothy.

"Some of it was terrible. Most of it was beautiful! But, Aunt Em, there's no place like home!"